Forsaken Trail

A Whitcomb Springs Short Story

MK McClintock

Copyright © 2018 MK McClintock
All rights reserved.
Trappers Peak Publishing
Bigfork, Montana

Published and printed in the United States of America

McClintock, MK
"Forsaken Trail"; short story/MK McClintock

Cover design by MK McClintock
Cover Image Background by Wollertz | Shutterstock
Cover Image Grizzly by wschwisow | Pixabay

For Grandmother.
Always in our hearts.

Forsaken Trail

A Short Story

Whitcomb Springs, Montana Territory
May 30, 1865

S HE NEVER IMAGINED dying at the hands—or paws—of a bear. Either she'd end up dead like the poor driver she hired in Bozeman or find a way to escape unscathed. Considering the layers of skirts and petticoats she wore, Abigail wasn't going to bet on her ability to outrun the great animal.

She remained still in the low branches of a tree. Unable to climb higher unless she removed her skirts, Abigail controlled her breathing so as not to alert the animal. The past few years of her life had been in pursuit of an education. Her work in the war relief had kept her busy for four long years, but she found time in the evening hours to consume knowledge. The more she learned, the more she wanted to know.

Abigail read most of the leather-bound volumes of

work in her family's library, from philosophy to geography to history, and everything in between. Unfortunately, not a single text had explained what to do when confronted by five hundred pounds of bear. Magnificent though the animal was, Abigail didn't want to become dinner.

Poor Mr. Tuttle had fallen from the wagon and broken his neck when the horses spooked and ran off. She'd been unable to drag him away, let alone pull him up a tree. Even now, she watched as the massive brown bear sniffed around the body. She dispelled a deep breath when she realized it wasn't going to eat Mr. Tuttle. It looked around instead, smelling the air.

Abigail swore it stared directly at her. Too late, she recalled that bears climb trees. Her first thought had been to escape, and unable to outrun the creature, she went up. She calculated if the bear stood on its back legs, it could reach the low-hanging branches where she hid and knock her from the tree with one swipe. She grabbed the nearest branch above her head and pulled herself up. Abigail ignored the loud rip in her skirt and the sudden gush of cool air that hit her legs and climbed higher. Two more branches put her out of swiping distance.

The grizzly sauntered toward her and stood, staring and studying. She imagined it thinking of all the ways it could rip her apart and savor her like a delicious meal. The stays on her corset would be no match for those great claws, and the teeth . . . Abigail shuddered and reminded herself that most living creatures weren't vicious by nature.

Abigail knew the animal was aware of her location. It landed back on all fours and approached the base of the tree. The heavy breathing and snorting filled the silence.

"I don't suppose we can work something out?" she called down to the bear, feeling foolish but not knowing what else to do. "Why don't you go your way and I'll go mine?"

Abigail covered her ears and pulled herself as close to the tree trunk as possible. The bear turned its head toward the sound of the gunfire before dropping on all fours. Another bullet hit the tree near the bear's head. The bear snorted again and after the third shot hit the ground a few feet away, the animal turned away from the tree and headed across the clearing to the forest. Abigail kept her tight hold on the branches and didn't look down when she heard the sound of a horse beneath her.

"If you can manage to climb back down, he's gone."

"Yes, but now you're here." Abigail thought she heard a chuckle. She dared a glance but couldn't see much of the man's face, shadowed by his hat.

"I can ride away if you prefer, ma'am, but there isn't another soul likely to come by today." After a minute of silence, she heard a loud sigh. "If you aren't coming down, the least you can do is explain what happened to Tuttle."

"You know—knew—Mr. Tuttle?"

The man below her didn't answer right away. She heard movement and saw he was no longer on his horse.

"I did. Looks like a broken neck."

She squeezed her eyes shut and asked, "Did the bear . . . make it worse?" She dared not ask if the bear tore the poor man apart.

Silence.

"Sir?"

Another chuckle. "No one calls me sir, ma'am. The bear probably figured Tuttle wasn't going anywhere. He was more interested in finding out what crawled up the tree."

"I didn't crawl!" Abigail realized the ridiculousness of her situation and studied the branches beneath her. The climb down wasn't too far. One of her petticoats was caught on a protruding branch. She shifted and the delicate fabric ripped even more. "I don't suppose you'll tell me the truth, but if I come down, will you promise not to harm me?"

"Interesting question seeing as how if I wanted to harm you, I'd've come up after you by now or shot you out of the tree straight away. The bear was more dangerous, and I gallantly, if I may add, chased the bear away."

"That's hardly reassuring." Abigial thought she'd kept her mumbling quiet enough for him not to hear, but she heard that damnable chuckle. "If you'd be so good as to move away, *sir*, I'll climb down."

"Go ahead."

Abigial lowered a foot to the next branch down, found her footing, and shifted her weight until she stood entirely on one branch. Only a few more to go, she told herself, unaware until now how far she had climbed up. She searched for the torn petticoat still caught, slipped, and fell before the shriek left her lungs. She landed with a soft thud, arms wrapped around her, and tangled skirts in her face. "Put me down!"

"Yes, ma'am."

Once on solid ground, Abigial stumbled away from her rescuer. She brushed hair from her face that had fallen from her once neat coiffure and straightened her skirts to preserve modesty. She saw only her outer skirt was torn, and most of her petticoat still intact. "I apologize. It was unkind of me to be ungrateful when you went to so much trouble . . ." Her eyes met his.

She imagined a woman in one of the silly romance stories her mother enjoyed. Heart fluttering, nearly out of breath, and eyes enraptured by the dashing gentleman. Only this wasn't a story and there was nothing dashing about the stranger before her. Dangerous, rugged, and beneath the days' worth of beard, a handsome man. She wondered if he kept his hair long to protect from the elements or detract from his striking features. Could a man be beautiful, she wondered? His blue eyes fascinated her so much she looked up to the sky to confirm they were the same color.

"Ma'am?"

"Excuse me, sir. I meant to express my gratitude. There is no excuse for my poor manners. You rescued me from that bear and I am in your debt." Abigail stepped forward, showing some of the moxie her sister possessed in abundance, and held out her hand.

When the stranger didn't reciprocate, she dropped her hand to her side. "My name is Abigail Heyward, and Mr. Tuttle was escorting me to Whitcomb Springs."

COOPER STARED AT the outstretched hand, gloved in white lace, now torn and dirty, with long and delicate fingers. He noticed beneath the fabric her skin was soft, like her face. His eyes moved to take in everything from her black, laced boots and torn skirt to the fallen tendrils of honey-colored curls. He had let go of her too soon, by her startled request, though he would have liked to have kept her close a while longer. Six long years since he last held a woman close, and this one stirred things inside him like no other had.

Shame she was Evelyn's sister, and in his mind, untouchable.

"Cooper McCord." He walked toward his horse and mounted.

"You're not leaving me here?"

"Correct, Miss Heyward. I promised your sister that I would see you safely to Whitcomb Springs, but I imagine Tuttle brought you up here on a wagon. If you'll wait here a few minutes, the horses won't have gone far."

"Wait!"

The gentlemanly thing to do would have been to take her into town and come back for the body, but he refused to leave a good man dead for scavengers to take turns at his corpse.

"Miss Heyward?"

"You know my sister?"

Cooper nodded. "After you sent that telegram from Chicago, I offered to fetch you, seeing as how I had business in Bozeman. Learned you'd already hired someone, but no one remembered who." He saw her digesting what he'd already said. "You should have expected your sister would have sent someone."

"I arrived earlier than planned and was impatient to reach town. Mr. Tuttle was for hire."

"He is at that, but not much of an escort." He started walking away again when her next words stopped him.

"May I come with you? I see how wrong it is to leave Mr. Tuttle here alone, but . . ."

Cooper studied her, knowing it wasn't wise to get too close. He watched her eyes, filled with apprehension, and wondered what made her decide to trust him. He held out his hand. She remained by the tree, and he said, "Stay or go with me, Miss Heyward, but I'm riding, not walking."

He watched her look at the covered body and make her decision. She inhaled and straightened her back, though he doubted it could get any straighter than before, and walked toward him. She clasped his hand and looked up.

"If you can manage, you put a foot in the stirrup."

Her incredulous expression told him that wasn't going to happen. Without asking permission, he reached down, grasped her underneath the arms, and pulled her into his lap. He ignored her startled reaction and waited for her to get settled.

He considered embarrassing her by mentioning the bright rosy hue rising in her cheeks, then thought better of it. The last thing he needed was to be too friendly.

"You followed us, I mean the wagon, back from Bozeman? I'm surprised we didn't meet on the road."

"I didn't come down the main road. There's a faster route, but it's not suited to wagons."

She leaned forward, separating her back from his chest, and he shook his head. Abigail said, "Evelyn and Daniel must trust you a great deal."

"They do." He left it at that and invited no further conversation. Cooper followed the wagon tracks with ease. The horses stopped in a meadow and grazed on spring grass. He saw no signs of predator tracks and counted the horses lucky. A quick inspection of the harness revealed one had loosened and a strap caught around one of the horse's legs. Blood trickled down over the animal's hoof. Cooper swore and dismounted. The other horse was uninjured but couldn't pull the wagon by itself, not weighed down as it was with two large trunks and two small trunks. Mr. Tuttle had secured them well with ropes and they had remained intact.

"Is she going to be all right?"

"Should be." He pointed to the trunks in the back. "Doesn't appear you lost anything."

"Possessions hardly matter when a man has lost his life."

Cooper studied her again, this time with admiration for more than her looks. On the outside, she appeared to be the beautiful, well-born eastern lady Evelyn had described, but Cooper wondered if there might be more beneath the genteel exterior. He remembered the first time he guided Daniel and Evelyn Whitcomb into these mountains. A year before war divided friends and family, the Whitcombs traveled west for adventure and a beginning. He mistook Evelyn for a pampered woman unable to fend for herself. When her husband joined the Union army, she proved him and everyone else wrong.

Cooper stayed close by while she continued to build a town and help people search for their own new beginnings. He might have found her attractive in the beginning, but it was her strength and determination he admired most. They'd become loyal friends who respected each other, and later close as brother and sister without the bond of blood.

What his body and mind experienced when he looked at Abigail was different, with no thought of friendship or brotherly feelings. Lust, attraction, and now confusion thwarted his more common sensibilities. He'd left a big city long ago because of a well-bred and spoiled woman, and he'd be damned to let his heart risk breaking over another one.

He tried to keep his thoughts off Abigail. He took care with the injured animal. He unharnessed the mare and hitched his own horse up to the wagon. A strong gelding, the horse stood a few hands taller than Tuttle's other mare, but there was no other option if Cooper was to get Tuttle and Evelyn's sister to Whitcomb Springs. He removed the semi-clean cloth from around his neck, wet it with fresh water from the canteen, and tied it around the mare's injured leg to help stop the blood flow. The animal needed rest and treatment, but Cooper didn't think it would go lame. He secured the mare to the back of the wagon and turned to Abigail.

"It's time to go." He regretted the curt tone as soon as he said the words.

"Are you angry with me?"

Cooper smoothed the lines on his face. *Had he looked angry?* "Not at all. I don't like to see any animal in pain. My apologies."

"Is that why you didn't kill the bear?"

His eyes narrowed as he faced her. "The bear might have tossed you about some if it got the chance, but more often than not they'd rather steer clear of people. It gave me no reason to kill it."

They sat in silence on the wagon bench while Cooper turned the team back to the road. He told himself not to look at her, to ignore her, but a proper upbringing would not be squelched, no matter how he chose to live his life. "Your sister was surprised when she received your last message."

He sensed Abigail's surprise, and she confirmed it when she said, "I sent a telegram. Surely she received it right away."

Cooper smiled. "We don't have a telegram just yet. Telegrams go into Bozeman or Butte, and depending on who it's for, it comes up by the mail wagon or a rider. Seeing as how a lot of folks know about Evelyn's generosity, they sent a rider."

"You know her well, using her Christian name."

"She's been Evelyn to me for a long time now."

"And her husband?"

Cooper did glance her way this time. Her body went rigid and her voice hard. "Don't go thinking what you're thinking, Miss Heyward. Your sister and her husband are my friends. I've known them a long time."

"Evelyn mentioned you in her letters."

"Which explains why you decided to trust me, after I told you my name."

Abigail nodded. "The family worried about her when Daniel left. She spoke of you fondly."

"She's a good woman. They're good people, Evelyn and Daniel."

"She also said you were a tracker and miner."

Cooper guided the horses around a rock in the road and made a mental note to return and clear it off the path. The road to Whitcomb Springs narrowed in some areas and widened in others. It went uphill and down and overrun with grass in places, but Cooper and others from town kept it passable for horses and wagons.

"I'm a lot of things, Miss Heyward."

"You don't sound or look like a mountain man."

He grinned and gently slapped one of the leather reins on the rump of the mare. "And you've met many mountain men, to know what they sound and look like?" Cooper admired the way her cheeks pinkened.

"No, I haven't. I've read stories, but I suppose it's not the same thing."

He remained silent as he recognized the place where Tuttle's body lay waiting.

"Are you a mountain man?"

"Like I said, I'm a lot of things." Cooper pulled the horses to a stop so the back of the wagon was near the body and stepped down. "You ought to stay up there, Miss Heyward, while I rearrange things in back for Tuttle." She did as he suggested. Cooper glanced her way every so often to make sure she looked anywhere except the body. Abigail Heyward had more gumption than he would normally credit a city woman. She hadn't fainted, screamed, or wept.

"You can leave my things here," she said without turning around. "It doesn't seem right for Mr. Tuttle to ride with my luggage."

When he had Tuttle situated in the back alongside her trunks, Cooper climbed back onto the seat next to her. "Tuttle would have been disappointed, considering the trouble he went making sure your trunks were safe."

"You say he was your friend, yet you don't appear upset by his death."

Cooper set the horses in motion, keeping a slow and easy pace for the sake of the injured mare trailing behind them. "Who's to say how I feel. I liked Tuttle well enough. He was a good man but an irritable sort. He was also drunk when he fell off the wagon, so I figure his death wasn't anyone's fault except his own."

"He was drunk?"

Cooper nodded, and they started on a gentle incline. "Smelled it on him. He held his liquor pretty good, but he knew better than to take a lady on a wagon ride before he sobered up." He noticed her alabaster cheeks turn rose again. "Something you're not saying, Miss Heyward?"

"I offered Mr. Tuttle a good sum to depart early. He said it would take a day, perhaps more, yet I was impatient. His death was my fault."

They reached a plateau and Cooper halted the horses. "It's not your fault. Tuttle knew better, you didn't. No sense in believing otherwise. Truth be told, it was bound to happen with him." He put the team back in motion and they rambled along. "He'll get a proper burial, Miss Heyward, and that's all he'd care about in the end."

"I give you leave to call me Abigail, please. Miss Heyward sounds far too formal for this wilderness."

Cooper repeated her name a few times in his mind and enjoyed the way it rolled off his tongue. "If you don't mind, I prefer Miss Heyward." He saw the flash of disappointment in her eyes and admired her all the more for not saying anything about it. No doubt in his mind, Abigail Heyward was trouble. The sooner he delivered her safely to her sister and brother-in-law, the better.

ABIGAIL DRIFTED BETWEEN frustration and gratitude. Those feelings shifted entirely to concern when Cooper stopped the wagon and said they couldn't go on.

"What do you mean?"

He pointed, and she looked ahead. A massive tree lay in the center of the road. On either side boulders taller than a man prevented passing. "Do we have to turn back?"

Cooper shot her a look, and she said, "Yes, I know, a foolish question. Obviously, a tree that size must take a great number of men to move. Is there another way around?"

"There is. As I mentioned before, I didn't come down this way so I did not see the downed tree on the road."

He jumped down and led the horses off the road. She waited while he hefted and carried large rocks from nearby and set them behind each wagon wheel. When he finished, he started to remove the harness from the horses.

"Mr. McCord. I don't mean to be difficult, and I'm sure you have far more important matters to attend than seeing me to town, which I truly appreciate, but what are you doing?"

"Unhitching the horses, Miss Heyward."

I'm not going to ask. I'm not going to ask. She asked

anyway. "And why are you unhitching the horses? If there is a way around—"

"We can't take the wagon the way we're going. Once I get a few men from town, we'll clear the road and I'll see your things are delivered."

"I don't care about my trunks, at least not too much. What about Mr. Tuttle, and the injured mare?"

"I'll bury Tuttle in a shallow grave, cover him with your trunks and the wagon, and bring him back to town after we move the tree. The mare can travel where we're going. The trail is passable but not wide enough for a wagon."

He sounded blasé, and she wondered what sort of man treated life and death with such a matter-of-fact approach.

When Cooper came around to her side of the wagon and offered to help her down, Abigail relented. Out of her element. That's what Evelyn would say, *did say* when she wrote back trying to convince Abigail not to make the journey west. Evelyn pleaded with her to wait until she and Daniel could meet her in St. Louis and travel the remaining miles to Montana. Abigail, in her impatience, set out with two cousins who were on their way to Chicago. She hadn't lied to them exactly though she failed to mention Chicago wasn't her final destination. As soon as she sent the telegram to Evelyn, she departed Chicago.

She trusted Cooper McCord. Even if her sister had spoken of him with high regard, she sensed somehow she could trust him.

"The mare can't carry any weight, so your belongings will have to stay with the wagon. I have room in my saddlebags for a few items you might want to take along now."

Abigail thought of the piles of clothes, books, and treasures she'd tucked away when she left home.

He interrupted her thoughts with a question. "How long are you planning to visit your sister? Appears by your luggage you plan to stay a spell."

"I don't know yet, Mr. McCord."

He hauled her trunks, one by one, from the bed and set them aside. It was then she saw Mr. Tuttle. "You don't want to be looking at him."

"I've seen dead men before."

He leaned on the back of the wagon and studied her.

She felt exposed beneath his gaze, yet unable and not wanting to make him stop.

"Where?"

"At the hospital. Men and boys sent home. Some survived, but many failed to recover from their injuries. I read to them, fetched water . . . they deserved much more than I gave."

"Your sister knew about this?"

Abigail shook her head and tore her attention away from the body. "No. Neither did our mother. My father caught me once but kept my secret."

"Why did you do it?"

"I needed to do . . . something. I'm not brave, Mr. McCord. I was no Florence Nightingale or Clara Barton in the heat of battle tending wounds and saving lives. I was grateful to live in the North, removed from the worst of the fighting. Many of our acquaintances enlisted and never returned home. I remained safe at home, praying for the war to end, for our lives to return to normal." Abigail turned and stared at the mountains all around her. "When it was over, I realized nothing would be the same, not for me. I couldn't go back to balls and parties, dress fittings and lavish dinners. I want to have a purpose."

"And so, you came here."

Cooper whispered the words, yet Abigail heard them and realized how much she had revealed.

"HOW LONG WILL it take to reach town?"

Cooper secured the worn leather bags to his saddle, thinking of the trek ahead. "We'll be there tomorrow morning."

"But you said Whitcomb Springs wasn't far from here."

"It's not, but it's already late in the day. Storm's coming and I'd as soon get you to town before it reaches us. The trail leads us out of the way a bit and curves back around toward town. There's a place to wait out the storm." Cooper walked to her and stopped next to her and the horse. "Do you know how to ride?"

"Very well, Mr. McCord. Though, I'll admit to a lack of education for—"

"Trail riding?"

"Yes. The rolling hills of home do not compare to your rugged mountains. Are you certain . . . never mind. We should be on our way, yes?"

Cooper watched her in fascination. He guessed she wanted to ask if they could stay with the wagon, but she didn't cry and demand him to make things easier for her. When she grabbed the saddle horn and attempted to pull herself, Cooper stepped up beside her and lifted her into the saddle. He said nothing and neither did she. He thought the silence was better while he attempted to sort out the mixed feelings he had about escorting her to town. He swung up onto the back of his gelding and looked at Abigail, who stared at him. She didn't look away.

"The mare will follow us. Keep a good hold on the reins but keep it loose, too. If she veers off the trail for any reason, you bring her back in line."

"Is the trail dangerous, Mr. McCord?"

"Everything here is dangerous, Miss Heyward."

"I do wish you would call me Abigail. We're quite alone, which is already improper according to the standards by which I was raised. If proper is your concern—"

"It's not." Cooper smiled and shook his head at her. "You have a nice way of speaking." He sighed and looked at the trail ahead of them. "When we get to town, you're Miss Heyward again." He kept his gaze on her until she nodded her agreement. Cooper could avoid saying her name altogether. Better to keep his distance than dream for the impossible.

An hour on the trail and Abigail wondered how Cooper knew where they were going. The horses plodded along, surefooted and relaxed, through tall grass. Every once in a while, Abigail spotted what could be a trail beneath them, before it quickly disappeared under more grass, fallen twigs, and pebbles. Her traveling companion remained silent except to occasionally glance back and see how she was doing. Surprisingly well, she thought to herself, though aloud she assured him she was fine.

When she realized the trail they followed led into a forest thick with trees that blocked out much of the sunlight, Abigail asked, "How often is this trail used?"

"Not often."

Frustrated, she tried again. "And you say it's passable all the way to Whitcomb Springs?"

"Last I checked."

Patience, Abigail. Patience is your friend. She recited the mantra a few times when he stopped the horses, startling her. The mare she rode stopped without direction from her and was content to munch on grass. "Why have we stopped? The horses?"

"Horses are fine."

"Then—"

"We'll be moving along again shortly." He reached into a saddlebag and pulled out what appeared to be dried meat. He dismounted and walked it back to her. "This should hold you over until we break for camp."

She accepted the offering and stared, dumbfounded. "Camp?"

Cooper took his time getting back on his horse. She saw him focus on the ground and then up in the direction they'd come.

"There's a meadow and a small trapper's cabin we'll reach before dark. It doesn't get used much, and it's not what you're used to, but it will keep the rain off and the critters out."

Abigail grew increasingly frustrated with her guide. She told herself that if hadn't come along, the bear might have mauled her. If he hadn't offered to escort her to town, she'd be left in the elements with poor, dead Mr. Tuttle until someone else happened along. No, she was grateful and wouldn't complain.

Abigail put all her trust in Cooper and followed him into the dark forest. She was surprised to discover peace and beauty within the darkness. Smatterings of light filtered through the thick branches and dew reflected the filtered rays. The fresh smell of pine and moss mixed with air purer than anything she'd breathed before was incredible. She relaxed and enjoyed the quiet, for even with Cooper and the horses close by, Abigail felt as though nothing else existed in her serenity.

The silence grew maddening. "Does the trail have a name?"

"Forsaken Trail."

"Sounds ominous."

He shifted, looked over his shoulder at her. Every time he did, she wanted to study him a little longer than his quick glances allowed. His voice comforted her, and as serene as her surroundings were, the silence became difficult.

As though he understood her problem, he said, "It was named by the Salish, or so it's been said. The story tells of a warrior who had won many battles against other tribes, but who also lost many of his own people in those same battles. He wandered the land, crossing tribal boundaries in an attempt to create peace among them.

"He fell in love with a Shoshone woman and returned to his people's land. They wouldn't accept her and he came here to these mountains. They lived alone. It is said he hunted this trail and made his home in the meadow. He named the trail to remember all those he lost, who bled into the earth, into the forsaken places where they never should have been."

Abigail pulled slightly on the reins to stop the mare, bringing Cooper's attention to her. "We need to keep going."

"Is the story true?"

"Most legends begin with some truth. You do not need to cry for them, Abigail. They have shed enough tears." He faced forward again and set his gelding in motion. The mare immediately followed, and Abigail remained silent, her thoughts on the Salish warrior and his wife, and on the quiet emotion she heard in Cooper's voice when he spoke of them.

Cooper led them from the forest a few hours later

and into a meadow. They'd stopped only once. Abigail disliked having to ask for that much consideration, but Cooper didn't appear to mind. Never had she met a more accommodating man. Most men of her acquaintance played the part of gentleman with practiced and precise skill. Cooper's manner and kindness came naturally, honestly, with no pretense.

When they stopped in front of the trapper's cabin— a shack with a lean-to attached to one side—Abigail wasn't sure she could dismount. Her stiff muscles ached when she shifted. Cooper had warned her not to ride sideways on a western saddle, but she refused to ride astride. Now she regretted her pride for propriety's sake.

Before she slid off, Cooper was next to her, lifting her down. Once her feet met the earth, his hands lingered on her waist for a few seconds longer than necessary. Neither of them spoke, and he left her standing there while he tended to the horses. The emotions he evoked were both confusing and real.

"Abigail."

She turned, surprised that he used her given name. Despite her permission and request, he hadn't used it since they left the wagon. "Yes?"

"I need to get the horses settled in for the night. You can go on and see if anything can be used. I've left a few things here from time to time."

Curious, Abigail pushed open the wooden door and stood outside while light and air entered the small room. Grateful for the foresight not to walk in right away, she peered inside. Dust covered every surface and cobwebs hung from corners. A drab canvas hung from one of the two narrow windows, and neither had glass in their frames. She imagined such a place didn't need glass windows. She took a tentative step inside and scrutinized the rest of the interior, what there was of it, and determined that she may rather sleep outdoors.

"It's been longer than I figured, since anyone has been here."

Abigail pressed a hand to her chest and spun around. Though no one else could have gained access to the cabin without Cooper's knowledge, she was still startled by his sudden appearance. "You move without making a sound."

He shrugged. "A necessary skill for living in these mountains."

"Evelyn wrote that you lived primarily in town, or nearby these past four years."

"True enough."

"And before then?" She doubted he was the type of man to open up about his past, but the more time she spent with him, the more inquisitive she became.

"Here and there." He crossed the room and tore the canvas from the window. "If you want to wait outside, I'll get this place cleaned up enough for sleeping."

Abigail looked around again. A single cot was pushed against one wall and a scarred table and one chair sat on the opposite side. "I wouldn't mind sleeping outside tonight."

She caught a grin that came and went on his handsome face. He said, "You ever sleep outside?"

"No."

He chuckled. "There's a storm coming and it will hit tonight. You can't be caught outside in the rain; your sister would never forgive me. The cot will do for you tonight, and I'll keep watch."

"Keep watch for what?" Cooper didn't answer, so she prodded. "Is there some danger I should know about?"

"Go ahead on outside and I'll call you in when it's ready."

Abigail wondered about the odd expression and wariness in Cooper's eyes when she left the cabin.

COOPER CARRIED IN two buckets of water, left over from the last rain, and wiped away as much of the dust as he could. The cabin was not a fitting place for

Abigail Heyward to stay or sleep in, but she hadn't complained. Evelyn was strong and sure and brave— now. When he first guided her and Daniel into these mountains, he doubted she would survive the first winter. She surprised him by thriving. Cooper never figured out what prompted him to remain behind after Daniel went to war.

He waited for Evelyn to return home to her family, yet she stayed, and so did he. Year after year he expected her to give up. Instead, she planted her gardens, hired men from all over to slowly build up the town and carve out the road to allow for supply wagons and travelers. When he discovered gold in one of the creeks near town, she put her trust in him and opened the mine.

Evelyn found her courage and remained in Montana. He remembered the doubt and fear in her eyes, yet every day she grew stronger and less dependent on him. Abigail was like her sister. If he hadn't come along, he believed Abigail would have figured out how to get past the bear and find a way to Whitcomb Springs. Perhaps she saw more of the war than she'd confessed to her sister. He shook his head from thoughts of the war and stepped outside into the shafts of narrow sunlight. Clouds rolled in and he estimated another hour before the first part of the storm hit.

"Abigail?" He called her name a second time, louder. "Abigail!" He ran around the small cabin, finding no sign of her. He returned to the front and looked down. Dainty boot prints had pressed into the grass and soft earth, leading toward the trees. His heart rate increased, and he followed her prints, shouting her name. When he crossed most of the clearing between the cabin and trees, Abigail emerged with a smile on her face and her arms burdened with twigs. She looked perfect.

She moved toward him, so far unaware of his worried state. "I confess that I don't know anything about fires or if the stove inside works. I thought . . ." Her eyes met his. "What's wrong, Cooper?"

"Don't ever do that again."

"I didn't go far. You've done so much and I wanted . . . to help."

Cooper lifted the twigs and branches from her arms. "You don't know what you're doing. It's not safe out here on your own. Once you're in town, you'll be your sister's problem. Until then, I'm responsible for you."

"You have no right to be angry with me." He heard Abigail following him as he started for the cabin. She continued to speak even though he didn't respond. "I'm grateful for you coming along when you did, Mr. McCord, but I didn't ask you to be responsible for me.

I could have stayed with the wagon and poor Mr. Tuttle until help came." Her boots pounded on the boards when she entered the cabin behind him. "It was not my intention to inconvenience you. Why did you bother with me?"

Cooper dropped the twigs and turned. "You're Evelyn's sister, and she's about the only family I have." He exhaled and told himself to calm down before he said anything else. "It wasn't safe to stay with the wagon. I wrapped Tuttle up the best I could, covered him with dirt and your trunks, but the critters are going to smell death and come looking. Anything from bears to wolves, and if they found us, they would have tried to make a bigger meal of us all."

Abigail blanched. "They're going to—" she stifled the reflex to gag "—eat him? Why did you leave him there? We could have put him on the other mare."

"The mare is barely going to make it to town. She can't take any weight, and I wasn't going to leave her wounded and unable to run away if wolves found her. Tuttle knew these mountains and his departed soul isn't going to think less of us for surviving."

Abigail lowered herself into the single chair. He hated seeing any woman scared. "We'll be in Whitcomb Springs tomorrow, then I'll return to the wagon with men and clear the road. It will be all right,

Abigail."

"Would we really have been in danger, if we stayed with the wagon?"

"Yes." It was the simpler answer, easier. Cowardly. "I'm not taking any chances. We aren't too far from town, but if you plan on staying out here, even for a long visit, you have to understand the realities. You could walk through the meadow next to your sister's house and happen up on a mountain lion or bear. Worse, a stranger who won't give thought to your screams."

Abigial shuddered, and he saw her shrink back. "You're a very blunt man, but I see your point. I wasn't doubting your decision to keep moving. If I am to stay—"

"If?"

"*If* I am to stay, I need to learn how to survive. I appreciate your patience with my inexperience."

He watched her stand and leave the cabin. The first rumble of thunder shook the heavy air. He continued to watch her through the open door. She stared into the distance though he couldn't see her face. Were her eyes open? What was she thinking? He asked himself these and many other questions, knowing answers would not come tonight.

THE FIRST SIGN of rain dropped on Abigail's nose. She'd discarded her hat to watch the sun set over the trees. The need to feel the cool breeze flow through her hair outweighed decorum. The simple act released her, for a few seconds, from the burden she carried with her. The heavy load of doubt about leaving home and her reasons why. Her mother called her impulsive and her father made sure she had plenty of funds to see her on her journey and for the shopping she planned to do in Chicago, where they believed she went. By now, her cousins would have sent word to her parents. She hoped her letter to them reached Pennsylvania first.

A few more drops hit her head and a spark of lightning coursed through the darkening sky. Clouds opened to reveal a small section of the galaxy, to showcase her flickering stars. It lasted only a moment before the wind blew the curtain of clouds closed. She sensed him watching her with those unreadable eyes. Abigail glanced upward once more and returned inside where warmth from the stove drove away the cold. He stirred something in an indented pot on the small, black stove. The scent filled the cozy room and reminded Abigail how long it had been since she'd eaten a full meal.

"The beans are about ready. I didn't have anything else except this and jerky in my saddlebags, but it will keep your stomach full until we reach town tomorrow morning."

He continued stirring the beans, his back to her. She approached him, determined that he look at her when she spoke to him. "Cooper?"

He looked up.

"I'm sorry."

"Nothing to be sorry for."

Thunder blasted through the air once again, followed by another flash of lightning. "Will it reach us?"

Cooper appeared to listen and then shook his head. "We should be fine."

"What about the horses?"

"The lean-to will keep them dry."

She accepted the plate of beans and spoon he handed her and noticed he didn't take any for himself. "You're not eating?"

"You have your fill. I'm going to check on the horses."

Abigail waited ten minutes before checking the silver watch fob attached to her outer breast pocket. She never went anywhere without the watch, a gift from her father. Ten minutes turned to fifteen when the cabin door opened and Cooper walked in, soaked through.

"It's coming down hard out there, but the thunder has stopped. Horses are secure for the night so long as the noise doesn't return. Scout doesn't mind too much, but Tuttle's mares are a mite skittish."

"Scout?"

Cooper stoked the flames in the stove. "My horse."

He didn't seem inclined to hold up the conversation, keeping his back to her as he did. Abigail succumbed to exhaustion and glanced toward the cot. A blanket not there earlier now covered the dusty mattress. Another lay on the edge.

"You should be warm enough tonight with the fire going. Try to get some rest."

Abigail sank onto the cot and spread a wrinkle from the blanket. "Thank you, Cooper."

Cooper nodded once and settled in the chair at the table. To her surprise, he withdrew a knife and a small piece of wood shaved down in places. Too weary to do anything except lay down, Abigail spread out over the blanket and drew the second one over her body.

The storm abated and sounds of the evening forest drifted through the open windows. The horses nickered a few times before quieting. Cooper whittled at the piece of pine, slow, easy movements downward, turning a simple piece of wood into a replica of his horse. He wished he had the skill to carve Abigail's face.

He moved his eyes every few seconds to study the soft lines of her cheek and the way her long eyelashes brushed the skin beneath her eyes. When an occasional soft moan escaped her lips, he would stop his hands and watch to make sure she was still asleep. He had nothing to offer a woman like Abigail Heyward.

For the first time since he left Boston ten years ago, a part of him wished he was still the type of man fit for such a woman. He'd met a few from larger cities who yearned for adventure and traveled to the open plains or high mountains, only to realize what they yearned for more than adventure was comfort and convenience. Evelyn was one of the first of her kind to stay and build a life in these mountains. Since she and Daniel founded Whitcomb Springs, others like her came and forged their version of new beginnings. He admired these women, yet still believed they were an exception.

ABIGAIL TURNED ONTO her back then faced him again, her eyes still closed. She moaned and cried out a name. "Jacob!" She swatted at the air around her for a second and appeared to calm down. Cooper was on his haunches next to the cot, there if she needed to be awakened. She thrashed, her arms connecting with his face. She said the name again, this time on a moan with tears cascading down her cheeks.

"Abigail, wake up." He held her arms so close so she couldn't hurt herself. "Please, Abigail. Wake up!" Cooper smoothed her hair back, and when he pulled away, his hand saw that it was damp from her sweat. He shook her gently until her eyes opened in a rush.

"Jacob!" She looked around as she exhaled one frantic breath after another. Her eyes met his and Cooper saw the exact moment when she realized he was real and she no longer suffered in the nightmare. "Cooper." She whispered his name and grasped his hand. "You're alive."

"I'm alive. I'm right here." He held onto her hand, never losing contact with her gaze. "You were having one heck of a nightmare."

She tugged at the top buttons of her travel jacket. He knew modesty prevented her from removing even her outer clothes before she fell asleep, but between the heat from the stove and the light wool of her fancy clothing, she appeared to be uncomfortably warm.

"I haven't had one in weeks. I'm sorry to . . . I'm sorry."

This is a bad idea, Cooper thought even as he wiped a few tears from her cheek. "Don't be sorry. Do you want to talk about it?"

Abigail shook her head and released his hand. He

rose so she could scoot to the edge of the cot. "The storm has stopped."

Cooper nodded.

"Is it safe to go outside for a few minutes? I just . . . need a few minutes."

By way of an answer, he opened the door for her. "Call out if you need me. I left a couple of buckets out front to collect more rain water."

She thanked him and stepped outside. He closed the door behind her. Meager though their privacy was, she deserved as much as he could give her. Cooper wiped both hands over his face a few times. He stopped himself from going to one of the windows when he heard her footfalls on the wet grass and twigs. He gave in and crossed to the opening in time to see her walk toward bushes still in the first budding. Winter had been long and spring late, making everything in their corner of the mountains lush and full. He moved away when she ducked out of sight. Cooper returned to the chair and his whittling.

A short while later the splash of water out front alerted him of her return. He didn't know why, but he sensed that opening the door for her, coddling her, wasn't what she needed or wanted. He understood her struggle and recognized the look in her eyes when she woke from whatever demons tormented her sleep. She wasn't in Montana only to see her sister. Abigail left behind more than family and carried the pain with her still.

She opened the door and stepped inside, saying nothing. He followed her lead and kept silent, even when she removed her tailored traveling jacket and laid it on the end of the cot. She spread herself out once more but didn't close her eyes and fall asleep as Cooper hoped she would. Instead, she looked directly at him.

"Have you always lived out west?"

He swept his knife smoothly over the wood's surface, away from his face. The new shredding joined the others on the floor at his feet. "No."

"Where are you from?"

Cooper tried to gauge her mood. Smudges of dark skin appeared under her eyes, shadows he suspected were there long before she decided to leave Pennsylvania. If she needed to talk, to forget whatever haunted her, he'd reveal everything about himself, even if the thought of doing so made him cringe. "Boston."

Surprise flickered in her eyes, though not an insulting surprise, more curious. "I visited there once. Why did you leave?"

He'd come a long way from those years in the city. "For a lot of the same reasons most folks come west. I was young and longed for adventure. I finished school and was set on a path my father approved of, but one I didn't want, so I left."

"And what did your father want for you?"

"The family business. Import and export, neither of which interested me." Cooper turned back to his piece of pine wood, smoothing a thumb over the surface. He had a way to go before it would look like Scout.

"If you're from Boston, why didn't you return home to fight in the war?"

And there it was, the question he guessed she really wanted to ask all along. When he didn't answer right away, she apologized and mumbled a "never mind." Cooper placed the wood on the table and sheathed his knife in his boot. The room seemed to close in on him and he needed space. He moved to stand by one of the windows and let the fresh air course over him. The clouds had cleared, leaving a celestial wonder of stars to gaze upon. "When I first left Massachusetts, it wasn't enough to get a little way from my father and the family responsibility. I went as far as I could without boarding a ship."

"The Pacific Ocean?"

Cooper smiled. "Not that far, but close. I went to California and made my way north. The Oregon and Washington Territories were created, and not long after several conflicts with the native tribes broke out.

I was foolish enough not to leave when I had the chance. I signed on as a civilian attached to the army. I kept records on everything that happened. As much as I wanted to leave, I had agreed to stay on until the end of the conflicts. I learned to shoot, hunt, track, and anything else that might help keep me alive. I wrote down every horrible thing each side did to the other, kept a journal of every man in the company who died, and did my best to keep a record of the other side's deaths."

Cooper sighed and gripped the rough edge of the window. "Hostilities broke out between the army and the Yakama people. A few deaths, broken treaties, rape, unruly prospectors, and the death of a man named Bolon of the Bureau of Indian Affairs, made a lot of people nervous. Both sides sensed an uprising and what followed . . . It took four years for them to sign a peace accord. What people are capable of doing to each other was something I'd never witnessed before that."

He turned around and faced her, leaning against the cabin wall. She sat up now, her feet tucked under her legs and the blanket wrapped around her shoulders. "I saw enough death to last me ten lifetimes. I couldn't watch brothers, friends, and countrymen slaughter each other. Don't get me wrong, those who fought for the right reasons are good and noble men. What it makes me, I don't know."

THIS TIME THE tears in Abigail's eyes weren't for herself but for Cooper. She hadn't expected him to reveal so much. No one talked of the war back home, at least around her, claiming she was too gentle. They wanted to forget, to go back to the way life was before the spring of 1865 brought the beginning of an end. She fought an internal battle about her reasons for leaving home. She avoided her parents' questions and had left the truth out of her letters to Evelyn. Yet she believed this man, this stranger she'd known for less than a day, would understand.

As though reading her mind, Cooper asked, "Why did you really come to Montana, Abigail?" He recited her name with reverence, as though savoring each syllable. "Who's Jacob?"

She wrapped the blanket tighter around her body and exhaled a shaky breath. "He was a patient at the hospital where I volunteered. He was from Virginia, a prisoner far from home and alive, barely, because a Union surgeon showed enough compassion to treat his more serious injuries before helping Union soldiers who came in on the same wagon.

"He was so young, eighteen two months before.

The war was almost over, but no one knew how close. He wanted to fight for his home so he joined. Two months later, he lay in the hospital. I read to him, sat with him when he was frightened, and wrote letters for him to his family. I don't know if they ever reached Virginia, but I promised him. He lived for two weeks, three days, and sixteen hours before he jumped out of a second-story window."

Abigail caught a movement and shifted her gaze to Cooper. He stood closer to her now but still kept a distance between them. She had to finish telling him, had to tell someone. "The Union doctor who operated on him and I were the only people there when Jacob was buried. No letter ever came back from his family. I learned after the war that their home had been burned, with them inside." Tears fell freely now.

Cooper cleared his throat before speaking. "You never told anyone."

She shook her head and swiped at the moisture on her face. Abigail tried to keep her body from shaking. "I mentioned how my father found out I volunteered at the hospital, but he didn't know I helped directly with the wounded. If he, or my mother, had . . . it's not that they're unkind, but they believed me too fragile. They were right." A shudder coursed through her body. When Cooper sat next to her and pulled her into his arms, she couldn't understand why until she recognized sobs coming from her. She gripped his arms and leaned into him, drawing from his heat, his strength, and their shared sorrows.

Abigail remained in his embrace until she had no tears left to cry. When she pulled back, their faces were a few inches apart, and she needed only to whisper. "You won't tell Evelyn, will you?"

She saw something akin to pain in Cooper's eyes when he answered. "No. You'll tell her in your own time, if you want to."

"Have you told anyone about those four years in Washington?"

"Not until tonight."

Abigail thought he might kiss her. They only met, but she would have allowed him the liberty. Instead, he brushed his fingers over her jaw and moved away.

"Think you could sleep a little now? There's only a few hours until daylight."

She nodded and lay back down. She fell asleep, imprinting his every feature to her memory.

SUN FILTERED IN through the open windows and a few cracks in the walls, waking Abigail from the few hours of restful sleep she'd managed to get. Sharing with Cooper had soothed the ragged edges of grief. Only time would heal her tattered soul, but at least now she believed an end to the misery was possible.

The horses snorted and Cooper's gentle voice, the one that soothed her last night, calmed the animals. Abigail hurried to get up. She folded the blankets and made use of the water in the bucket Cooper must have brought in while she slept. When she opened the door, she found Cooper hunched next to the injured mare, his hand moving up and door her rear leg.

"How is she faring?"

He must have heard her come out because he didn't look up. "She should be okay. Might not carry weight again, but she'll live. The girl deserves a rest." When he stood, he faced her.

Cooper didn't bring up her middle-of-the-night confession and tears, and neither did she. "How long will we ride today?"

"A few hours."

He was back to being taciturn, offering only those few words in response. Cooper rested a hand on the back of the mare and stared at her. If she knew him better she'd think he was annoyed; her parents always found her endless questions a nuisance. But she didn't know him better.

Abigail unconsciously clutched a fist at her breast

and looked around. "The mountain lion or the bear worried you last night, didn't they? You said you were going to keep watch."

"The animals go where they want. If one gets too close to town or livestock, we do what we have to, but I never hunt an animal for sport or because it's easier. Most of the time we can track it away from where we don't want them, but it doesn't mean they won't return." He patted the horse's rump and said. "We need to be heading out now."

Abigail nodded her understanding and started for the trees. "I will hurry. And Cooper? Is it always about life and death here?"

His eyes darkened and for a second, she thought she saw sadness in them. "It's life and death everywhere."

THREE HOURS OF silence later, Cooper led their small party of two, plus one extra horse, into Whitcomb Springs. He was a man of few words and he'd already said more than he ever had at one time to anyone. He wanted to bring up last night so many times. Instead, he kept quiet and allowed her to enjoy the magnificent scenery. Every once in a while, he glanced back to find her eyes closed and a smile on her lips as she tilted her face back to the sun.

She took his breath away and made his heart ache for wanting what he shouldn't want. He remembered his father saying something similar about Cooper's mother. Thaddeus McBride may have been a dictator of a father, but he loved his family and adored his wife. Cooper never understood how one woman could affect a man so deeply—until now. He managed to go through thirty-two years of life without love. He figured he could last another thirty-two. A man couldn't lose what he didn't have. Townspeople waved and shouted hellos as they passed. Cooper had been a fixture in the town since the first cabins and trading post were erected. He liked belonging somewhere and only realized it now as he looked upon familiar faces and welcoming smiles. Evelyn and Daniel likely told a few people of her sister's impending arrival. Still, they'd be curious about the trail-weary lady in the city clothes, speculate among themselves as to why she came west.

He turned them right on another road, passed the general store and hotel. The Whitcomb's house stood out above the rest, as tall as the hotel that rarely saw guests. Evelyn insisted on a hotel, not just a boarding house. She predicted one day enough folks would get in their heads to pass through their town.

"Cooper?"

He indicated to his horse, with a gentle tug on the

reins, to hold back. When Abigail's mare came alongside his, they continued on.

"Is that Evie's house?"

Cooper smiled, recognizing the shortened name Daniel sometimes used when speaking of Evelyn. "Daniel made sure it was finished before he left."

Abigail looked around in amazement. "She imagined all of this?"

"She did. Stubborn lady, your sister. I have a feeling you take after her in that way."

Abigail turned to him and he grinned to let her know he was teasing. She returned his smile and for a moment they were happy just to be alive and together. When the front door of the house opened and Evelyn shouted her sister's name, the moment passed and Cooper dismounted. He walked around his horse and put enough room between the animals to help Abigail down. If his fingers lingered longer at her waist than they should have, she said nothing of it.

Evelyn hurried through the open gate and ran to her sister, pulling the shorter woman into a fierce and loving hug. "When I saw you from the window riding in, I couldn't believe it." Evelyn stepped back and directed her next question to Cooper. "How did this happen?"

Abigail drew her sister's attention. "I'll explain

everything, Evie, I promise." She jumped a little with delight when she saw Daniel approach and embraced him as she would a brother. "You look like a farmer," she said with a wide grin.

"We're clearing more land to put in an orchard. How are you Abbie, girl?"

"Perfect."

Evelyn slipped an arm around Abigail's waist. "First thing, a bath, and then I want you to tell me everything. You, too, Cooper."

Cooper enjoyed witnessing the family reunion. He was an only child and never knew the bond of a sibling. He envied them. "I have to feed and water Scout then head back out. We left a wagon with Mr. Tuttle at the bend by the large oak." Cooper hated reporting a death. "Tuttle didn't make it. He was driving Miss Heyward here. It's a long story, but the telling of it will have to wait or be done without me. I need to get back and take a few men. A tree's blocking the main road, and we couldn't get the wagon through."

Evelyn's face bore various expressions from surprise to sadness all wrapped in a layer of curiosity. Daniel said, "I'll come with you, Cooper."

"Shouldn't you—"

"I'm coming."

Cooper guessed Daniel not only wanted to help,

this being his town, but he'd get the story faster from him than if he waited for Abigail's retelling of events. "Appreciate it. I'll get a few more men and meet you at the blacksmith's. I have a horse here that needs tending."

When Cooper turned his horse around and started walking away, he heard his name. He also heard Abigial whisper something to her sister and Daniel. A second later she stood next to him.

"Were you going to say goodbye?"

"I'll be back tomorrow, Miss Heyward."

He saw the hurt in her eyes. He'd told her when they reached town she'd be Miss Heyward again. It had to be this way, he told himself.

She held out her hand. "Thank you, Mr. McCord." She added in a whisper, "For everything." Abigail returned to her sister and brother-in-law, and Cooper walked away without looking back.

AN HOUR LATER, after a warm bath and slipping into clothes Evelyn laid out on the guest bed, Abigail felt more herself. Evelyn stood three inches taller than her and the skirt hung a little low to the ground, but after what she'd been through to get her, clean rags would have sufficed. Abigail came downstairs to find her sister alone in the kitchen setting up their tea.

Evelyn set a teapot on the tray and glanced up. "You look more yourself. How do you feel?"

"Better, thank you." Abigail looked around at the beautiful home. It was a third the size of their family home in Pennsylvania, and Abigail adored it. It felt like a home rather than a showpiece. Their house had always been a happy place, at least before the war, but they'd never gone into the kitchens or attics, considered strictly servant domains. "If mother could see you now."

"She taught us to serve tea."

"Serve it once it was brought in and carefully arranged by a servant. You look wonderful, Evie. Happy. How marvelous it must be to have Daniel home."

Evelyn blushed and said, "Let's go into the parlor and enjoy our tea. The gardens are in their first bloom, and we can enjoy them more from there."

Abigail followed her sister into the cozy room with lots of light shining through the windows. She may not know what it takes to build a house, but Abigail recognized expensive when she saw it. Though modest compared to their upbringing, everything from the solid walls and thick carpets on the floors to the furnishings and china spoke of comfort and elegance.

"This is what you've been spending your money on." She accepted one of the fine china teacups and sipped the hot tea. "I approve. So, would Mother and Father."

Evelyn said nothing until she fixed her own tea and took the seat opposite Abigail. "I considered easing into this conversation, but I find I cannot. You can't know how happy I am to see you, Abbie, but why the rush to leave home?"

"I told you I wanted to visit."

"Yes, later. When I received your note from Chicago, I almost wrote Mother and Father to find out what happened. It's a dangerous journey through the territories. However did you get so far on your own?"

Abigail prepared herself for the questions, and she wondered if Cooper and Daniel were having the same conversation as they rode to fetch poor Mr. Tuttle. She set her cup on the table between them. The fine Irish linen bore no stains or wrinkles. "How do you manage all of this on your own?"

"There are two women who help out inside and the gardens. Harriett is helping at the general store today and Tabitha is looking after a neighbor who has a sick child. Please don't change the subject, Abbie. I need to know what's happened back home. You lied to Mother and Father when said you were going to Chicago."

"I'm not putting you off, Evie. I needed time to find

the courage to tell you."

"You've traveled thousands of miles. This should be the easy part."

"Not when you've heard everything." Abigail sat forward on the plush chair with its beautiful plaid cloth. "Mother and Father know by now. I wrote them when I was in Chicago. I will tell you all of it, but please don't interrupt and don't scold me until I've finished." Abigail spent the next thirty minutes repeating every event from the time she left their cousins in Chicago to how Mr. Tuttle died, the bear, Cooper finding her, and their journey up the trail to Whitcomb Springs. She told her all of it, except the private story about Jacob that she shared with Cooper or his own story. Those secrets she kept close and unspoken. "I love our parents, but they wanted to go back to the way things were before the war. So many friends of ours died and others returned crippled or depressed. I needed a change, Evie. Surely you understand."

Evelyn remained silent for several minutes, making Abigail nervous. She did not require her family's approval for her choices, but she and her sister had always been close, and Abigail despaired disappointing her. Chirping birds and the distant sounds of people going about their lives broke through the quiet. She enjoyed the view of the gardens and the mountains beyond the glass windows, covered in green pines and topped with snow. Abigail marveled at their height and beauty. She imagined waking up every morning to see those mountains and inhale the crisp air, which was nothing like the heavier, humid air back home. "I do understand. Have you told me everything?"

Abigail didn't want to lie. "No, but please accept there are things I'm not ready to tell you."

"Promise me that you'll tell me when you are ready. I know what it is to hold something inside. I was blessed those four years. You wrote me often and listened to my worries, and Cooper was here for me, when I needed to speak to someone."

"Yes, Cooper is a good friend."

Abigail shifted uncomfortably under her sister's quiet perusal, but no admonition came.

Evelyn said, "When you do write home again, be sure to leave out the tales of your recent adventures."

"I will." Abigail bore no regrets for the stormy night she spent tucked away in the cabin with Cooper. They both needed to share their sorrows, and in their giving of secrets, a bond, deep and lasting, had formed. The senseless loss of life on both sides still haunted him, just as Jacob's death haunted her. "He was a gentleman, Evie."

The statement required no answer, but Evelyn said,

"Abigail, I don't mean to scold, and you'll come to learn that proper doesn't always have a place in this wilderness. In your situation, you did everything I would have. Cooper's only concern was for you. That's the kind of man he is."

"He's a good one, isn't he? Like Daniel."

Evelyn smiled, her eyes brightening with moisture. "Yes, like Daniel."

DANIEL RETURNED THE next morning after the men went to clear the road and fetch Mr. Tuttle. They buried him in the town cemetery next to the church by the creek. It was a peaceful place with views of the meadow and mountains beyond. When she'd asked if the animals left Mr. Tuttle alone, Daniel refrained from going into detail and Abigail decided she'd rather not know. When she mentioned Cooper must be busy, Evelyn gave her an odd look and said nothing. Three more days passed before Abigail saw Cooper again.

Abigail needed to get away from the house for a little while. She visited every business in town—the few open businesses—and let her sister explain their plans for growth. Evelyn told her they'd sent out advertisements for a doctor and sheriff, with many more responses for the sheriff position. Abigail imagined the difficulty of finding an educated and licensed doctor to leave a hospital or private practice to come so far away from cities and amenities. The tour of the town resulted in meeting a variety of wonderful men, women, and children, though she remembered only a few names.

Despite the small population, Abigail found herself in need of alone time. She wanted to explore on her own and promised Evelyn she would stay close enough for them to hear and see her. Abigail accepted her sister's protective nature, and at one time welcomed it. No longer. She'd witnessed too much to go back to being the naive girl sheltered from life's horrors. She followed the stream where she found the deer path Daniel had mentioned. The path continued along the flowing water until it widened into what her brother-in-law explained would eventually become a river feeding into a lake. Abigail wanted to see it all.

She happened upon a trio of deer grazing and made herself comfortable on a large boulder next to the stream bank. They looked up once and continued eating the lush grass, unperturbed by her presence. An unfamiliar sound came from above and Abigail tilted her head back to search the sky. An eagle, with a wing span she'd never seen before on a bird, soared above. It circled twice before flying away and landing in a distant tree. Abigail laid back on the rock, spread her arms, and stared into the cloudy sky. She longed to be free as the eagle.

COOPER CAME UPON her with her arms spread wide and the hint of a smile on her face. He'd gone first to the house, searching for her, begging Evelyn without words to not ask any questions. It was Daniel who pointed to where Abigail ventured, and soon he found her. He waited, allowing her the peace she obviously felt and needed. He struggled for three days wanting to go to Abigail, to explain why he left the way he had, and each day he stayed away. He withdrew from town when they brought Tuttle's body and wagon back. He watched the funeral from a distance, though his eyes remained focused on Abigail. Her fancy clothes suited her even if they were out of place in the wild surroundings.

Three days and he gave in, unable to keep away any longer. Whenever he closed his eyes, he saw all the men he watched die and many he helped bury. Only now, those images faded, to be replaced by the wounded look in Abigail's eyes when he left. No one had managed to churn his emotions the way she did. He had to see her at least once more.

He noticed the twig on the deer trail and stepped on it, bringing Abigail to a sitting position. Her eyes widened at first, but he was uncertain about what he saw next. Confusion? Joy?

"You stayed away."

Cooper covered the distance between them in a few strides. He removed his hat and sat down next to her on the boulder, facing her. "I shouldn't have."

"Why did you?"

The deer, disturbed by their voices, scattered across the meadow. "I needed time to think."

"You came back. Evelyn said you would."

"This is home. I'll always come back."

"Have you stayed away because of me? Daniel seemed surprise not to see you around."

"I come and go, more so since Daniel returned." His heart's beat increased every time he evaded the topic that brought him out here, searching for her. "I'm not good with words, Abigail."

She shifted slightly to look at him more directly. The move brought her hand closer to his. "You could try."

He chuckled and pointed to the eagle above. It left its perch and now flew over them toward the mountains. "I understand him better than I do people. The land, these mountains, the animals, make more sense to me than the words I've been trying to figure out how to say. I could try to say them, but I suppose they won't come out right."

Abigail pleased him when she slipped her hand under his and linked them skin to skin. "We knew each other for one day and one night. It's not enough time for anyone to know a person."

"No, it's not. I'd like to know you."

He sensed her trembling nervousness, and with his words she relaxed. "I thought you were going to say something else."

"I was." Cooper squeezed her hand. "I had planned to leave. I came to see you one last time, to say goodbye to Evelyn and Daniel."

"And to me?"

"No." With his free hand, Cooper took a risk and cupped her cheek against his palm. Her skin warmed beneath his touch. "I couldn't say goodbye to you."

"You said you planned to leave. And now?"

He smiled and dropped his hand to her other side. "And now I'm not. I'm not the man my father hoped I'd become. That man is someone who might have deserved you. I don't, but I sure as hell am going to do my best. I want to know you, Miss Abigail Heyward. That is, if you're staying."

Abigail leaned closer to him. "Evie and Daniel are

likely watching us, but I don't care. I'm staying. I don't want to go back to an existence of parties and charities and dinners with people bejeweled in too much finery. Those days for me are gone. I experienced a lifetime in our day and night together and I want more of it. Yes, Cooper McCord, I'm staying. And I want to know you, too."

Cooper released a shuddering breath and brought Abigail's hand to his lips. "We have a lot of learning to do about each other."

She brought their joined hands to her heart. "We have time."

The End . . . and their beginning.

Thank you for reading "Forsaken Trail"! I hope you enjoyed the story; there's more to come.

Don't miss out on future books and stories in the Whitcomb Springs series:
www.mkmcclintock.com/newsletter.

Interested in reading more by MK McClintock?

The Historical Western Romance
Montana Gallagher series:
Gallagher's Pride
Gallagher's Hope
Gallagher's Choice
An Angel Called Gallagher
Journey to Hawk's Peak

Historical Western & Western Romance
Crooked Creek series:
"Emma of Crooked Creek"
"Hattie of Crooked Creek"
"Briley of Crooked Creek"
"Clara of Crooked Creek"

Historical Romantic Mystery
British Agent series:
Alaina Claiborne
Blackwood Crossing
Clayton's Honor

Enjoy her collection of heartwarming Christmas short stories any time of the year: *A Home for Christmas*

THE AUTHOR

AWARD-WINNING AUTHOR MK McClintock is devoted to giving her readers books laced with adventure, romance, and a touch of mystery. Her novels and short stories take you from the rugged mountains of Montana to the Victorian British Isles, all with good helpings of daring exploits and endearing love stories. She enjoys a peaceful life in the Rocky Mountains where she is writing her next book.

Learn more about MK by visiting her website and blog: www.mkmcclintock.com.

Made in the USA
Las Vegas, NV
07 November 2022

58992833R00042